'Aisling'

Emma-Jane Leeson

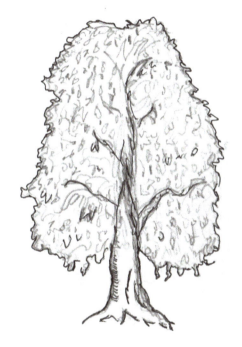

Created by The Johnny Magory Co. Ltd

First published 2020 by The Johnny Magory Company Limited.

Ballynafagh, Prosperous, Naas, Co. Kildare, Ireland

For Davey.

For living with a dreamer.

For helping her follow them.

Chapter 1.

You come here Knowing what you Wanted. Don't forget that...

"It's so dark in here" moaned Aisling again.

"Shh Aisling!" replied everyone annoyed.

"I just can't wait to get out of here and travel the world" she yearned.

Ever since the day she opened her eyes inside her growing conker shell, Aisling had been listening to the stories from the birds and animals who used her mother's great branches as their home.

Their stories of adventure, of danger, of fun from one landscape to another. Everyday Robin and Red Squirrel perched above her shell and answered all her endless questions about where they had been; who they had met; and what they did that day.

Aisling longed for the day she could get out of her shell and have her own adventures.

She dreamed about meeting lots of different animals, seeing different landmarks and parts of the landscape.

The other conkers were getting quite fed up with her constant longing and questioning.

Her mother just smiled and sent a loving feeling down through her branches when Aisling excitedly told her about her plans.

On a very rainy Sunday in September, Aisling was bored because it was too wet for her friends to come visit her.   "I can't wait to visit a beach" she said out loud. "I've heard they are beautiful; I wonder what the sand will feel like? Oh and of course the mountains sound wonderful too; all those steep hills and waterfalls. Red Squirrel really has me excited for that adventure" she continued.

"Oh, it's so dark in here" she complained loudly again but one of her brothers had had quite enough.

"Shut up Aisling!" he shouted, startling everyone on the branch. "You're a conker, a tree. You can't travel, you won't have adventures. Life is not fun!" he screamed, shaking with temper.

"You're going to fall from this branch like the rest of us. If you are lucky, that Red Squirrel might bring you and bury you in a hoard somewhere far away from us; but that's it. You'll stay there forever and ever; the end!" he shouted at the top of his lungs, out of breath.

Everyone gasped including her mother; but nobody said a word.

All that could be heard that afternoon were the drops of rain on the branches, leaves and grass below, and the soft sobbing of a heartbroken conker.

Chapter 2.

It's your life
Live it your
Way...

The next day the rain had stopped, and Aisling's friends came to visit her.

"Go away" Aisling said to them. She felt so stupid. She did not want to speak to anyone ever again.

Every time an adventure popped into her head, she quickly tried to push it out and not think about it.

The branch was incredibly quiet for the next few weeks and Aisling's friends stopped visiting her because she would not talk to them.

As her mother's leaves changed colour Aisling tried so hard to accept her life as her brother had said. Buy try as she might, she could not get the longing for adventure out of her head.

"I suppose being a tree like my mother will be fine" she thought to herself. "I'll still have my friends to talk to and give them shelter and homes; but oh, I just wish I could be different."

One crisp October morning, Aisling heard funny sounds coming from outside her shell. Heavy plops and drops on the ground below, much heavier than rain drops.

Suddenly, she heard a little 'crack' from the top of her own shell. All at once, she was filled with the most wonderful, amazing feeling she had ever felt.

For a few seconds, she was free.

She was moving.

She was falling from her mother's great branches.

For those few seconds, her wildest adventures lit up inside her head again and she felt as though she would burst with excitement.

The loud 'thud' when she hit the cold, frosty grass was actually enough to make her burst.

For the first time ever, she could see the world.

The brightness hurt her eyes, but they soon adjusted. "Wow" she gasped as she tried to make sense of all the wonderful objects, shapes, and textures around her. She gazed back up at her mother. Her height and size gave her a little shock, but her mother just smiled back at her.

Either side of her mother she could see a row of trees; oaks, ash, holly, hawthorn, birch, forming the boundary of a barley field. She turned her eyes to see behind her, a black tarmacked country lane with yellow road markings lay there. In the distance behind her mother she could see an old church ruin standing lonely amongst a giant field of stubble.

Aisling felt amazed under that bright blue sky.

Suddenly a feeling of warmth covered her. She turned around to see the fuzzy red whiskers and kind eyes of her friend the Red Squirrel for the first time.

"Are you ready for your first adventure Aisling?" Red Squirrel asked the beaming solid, beautiful brown conker.

"Oh, Red Squirrel, I'm so sorry I stopped talking to you" she sheepishly replied.

"I just felt so stupid and I didn't know..."

"Shh Aisling" Red Squirrel replied in a warm tone.

"I asked if you were ready for your first adventure, so answer me! Are you ready?"

Aisling smiled the biggest smile she had ever smiled and nodded.

With that, Red Squirrel picked her up and placed her gently in his mouth. He took a mighty leap up onto her mother's first branch then glided from branch to branch, tree to tree, climbing, running, and jumping.

Aisling could not talk; she had no words. She just watched and felt her heart soar. The most wonderful feeling she had ever felt. This was her first real adventure.

Chapter 3.

Surround
yourself with
those who
bring you
joy. Who
love & lift you
up...

That night, Aisling felt exhausted but full of joy as she talked and talked and talked to Red Squirrel; snuggled up beside him in his dry and warm drey. He had shown her so much that day. They went through O'Grady's farmyard. Aisling adored the cute young Friesian cows that were bucking and playing in the fields. He brought her to the lake to meet the Whooper Swans who had just arrived from Iceland for the winter months.

She seen the bog from a distance and most importantly met her friend Robin.

She could not remember falling asleep that night, but she could remember her amazing dreams when she woke the next morning. Red Squirrel's drey was in a silver birch tree in the hedges that formed around a pretty green bungalow. The garden of the house was filled with all kinds of trees and plants with a beautiful rope swing hanging from the branches of the study oak tree. There were swings, a slide, a big green trampoline, and a little timber house covered in ivy in the garden too, all brightly painted.

That morning Red Squirrel told Aisling he must go gather up some food for his hoard before the harsh winter came.

He took Aisling down from the drey and gently placed her on the ground at the bottom of the birch. He told her he would be back in a few hours. Aisling was happy to sit in the sun looking into the garden of the pretty green bungalow and thinking about yesterday's wonderful adventures.

She was basking in the warm sunlight that sneaked through the branches of the trees when she heard a gentle thud coming from the house. She opened her eyes to see a little human girl skip away from the door she had just walked out and shut behind her.

The girl was merrily singing a song as a friendly big brown dog came over to greet her. The girl wrapped her arms around the dog's neck and said "Morning Grouse" to him.

"Did you have a good sleep? I did" she spoke to the dog.

"Today I'm going to have an adventure in the garden, so you are my Chief Explorer ok?" Grouse just wagged his tail and snuggled his head into the little girls shiny red raincoat.

A black and white cat walked up to the girl and the dog and rubbed its body along the girl's blue welly boot.

"Morning Whiskers" said the girl to the cat as she bent down to rub him.

"I was just telling Grouse that today's adventure is in the garden. He's the chief explorer and I need you to be our Wild Cat and protect us from pirates ok?"

The cat purred loudly and slowly leaned his weight against the girl's leg, then turned his head and pushed it gently into her boot.

Aisling watched on in awe as the girl, her dog and her cat had fun in the warm October sun. Jumping, rolling, hiding, climbing trees. It was so exciting to watch. Aisling never spoke a word, just watched on with happiness and wonder.

"And now to find treasure Grouse" she announced when she came out after her lunch. "We need to find the enchanted wand, the philosopher's stone, the wisdom acorn and the magic pinecone" she instructed Grouse and Whiskers as she began pacing and searching the garden.

"Ah ha!" she shouted as she held up a glistening, round, whitish stone in her little hand. "The Philosopher's stone! Whiskers keep watch! This stone lets us see the future; the pirates have wanted it for years" she said putting the stone into the pocket of her red raincoat. Stooping low, herself and Grouse continued searching for and finding the items on her list as Whiskers sat on the branches of the willow tree fast asleep!

Aisling was delighted when the girl found her final item, the magic pinecone not too far away from where she was watching.

Aisling was so lost in happy thoughts and feelings she did not notice the girl walking closer to her spot. The girls high-pitched squeal brought her back to the moment.

"Wow Grouse look!" she exclaimed. "This is the most prized treasure of them all" she shrieked with excitement as she gently bent down and picked up Aisling in her warm, sticky hand.

She held Aisling up high in her outstretched arm facing the sun as she admired Aisling's shiny, marble-like shell.

"The mighty conker protects us from all evil. I can't believe we found it!" and with that she hugged Aisling close to her chest, looked at her once more then dropped her into her warm, red pocket.

Red Squirrel looked on from his drey smiling.

Chapter 4.

Every day is a
new Adventure.

From that day on, life was one adventure after another for Aisling and her friends the hawthorn stick, the acorn, the stone, and the pinecone.

Every night, they were carefully placed on the windowsill next to the little girl's bed while she slept. Then every morning she happily put them in her pocket and away they went.

Even in Aisling's wildest dreams, she never thought she would do and see as much as she did. School, supermarkets, playgrounds, restaurants, the houses of friends and family.

Every weekend, Aisling went somewhere new. A new park, a forest, pet farms and even mountains and the beach.

Life was better than she could have ever dreamed. Her new friends were just as grateful for their lives and Red Squirrel was so happy for her every time they got to talk in the garden.

Aisling was having so much fun she did not realise she was gradually getting weaker until one night on the windowsill pinecone exclaimed that her seeds were falling out all over the place because she had begun drying out and opening.

Acorn then said that he hadn't been feeling great either.
When Aisling heard this, it drew attention to her own self. She realised how weak she had become.

Looking at her reflection in the window, she saw that her beautiful shell no longer shone hard and bright but was now dull and soft in spots.

"What's happening to me?" she thought. Just then she felt a crack appear on her back.

"Acorn help me" she whispered afraid.

"I can't Aisling, the same has just happened to me" he barely whispered back.

She was so afraid.

Her eyes became heavy, her heart began to sink.

She looked at her friends for one last time as her eyes closed shut and a long sigh escaped her lips.

Chapter 5.

Even when it's dark, there's always light somewhere.
You just need to look for it in different ways.

Weeks had passed when Aisling finally woke in a dark, tight space. She could not talk or see and felt scared.

"Where am I? Am I back in my shell? Why is it so dark? Am I dead? Where are my friends? Oh, I wish my friends were here? I wish I was safe on the windowsill or in Red Squirrel's drey. I can't even open my mouth to talk, what's going on?" Aisling thought.

To distract herself she began to hum songs, happy songs that the little girl used to sing.

The humming made her feel a little better. Then she realised she actually was feeling a little better than the last night on the windowsill.

She was deep in thought and mindlessly humming when she faintly heard someone else humming with her not too far away. She stopped and the humming continued somewhere beside her.

This gently humming made Aisling feel better at least she knew she was not alone.

She thought she recognised the hum but wasn't sure.

She hummed along for hours with her mystery accompaniments until a familiar voice interrupted them.

"Good morning guys"

It was her little girl. Aisling's heart nearly exploded with excitement.

But her voice sounded muffled and Aisling could not see anything, let alone her smiling face. "Am I permanently blind?" she thought.

Suddenly she felt a cold sticky feeling overcome her "What on earth is that?" Aisling thought.

"So today I'm off to school, mam said I can't bring you guys in case I damage you so I suppose that's fair, but I would love to. So, it's just you and me philosopher's stone. I'll fill you guys in after school" said the little girl. Then Aisling felt the sticky cold feeling once more.

"Oh, I do hope you are all ok in there and I don't have to wait too long" the girl longed.

Aisling felt so comforted hearing the girls voice, but she did not know what was going on.

"Is this my new life?" she thought. "Well at least I can hear her voice" she consoled herself.

"And don't have to wait too long for what?" Aisling wondered.

Weeks passed. Aisling was feeling much better and began settling into her new life. She spent the days humming with her mystery choir and listening to the little girls stories every morning about her dreams and every evening about school.

But then one day, something happened that took Aisling by surprise.

Her little girl was chatting away as usual and Aisling could feel the sticky cold thing on her. Suddenly the little girl screamed, nearly frightening the life out of Aisling!

"Oh, mighty conker, I see you! You're growing" she exclaimed, and Aisling could feel herself move around through the air spinning.

"Oh, I'm so happy you're ok and you're out and I can see you again"

Aisling tried to open her conker eyes, but it was the same as always, she could not. Then she could feel something like a distant tickle.

She had never felt anything like it but with every touch the feeling was getting stronger and stronger.

Aisling followed the unusual feeling then suddenly, woah, she could see again!

The brightness took some time to adjust to. Her new eyes took a bit of getting used to but as the haze turned to focus, right there in front of her was the beaming, beautiful face of her little girl.

The most amazing fuzzy warm feeling flooded over Aisling. Her heart was singing again.

Chapter 6.

Life was great again. It was a little different as Aisling no longer fitted in the little girls pocket with her pals but herself and her friends, the acorn, the pinecone and the hawthorn stick now happily sat in their pots on the windowsill during the day while the little girl and the stone went to school.

Every evening and at the weekends, the little girl carefully put the pals on a special black and red tray that her grandmother had given her and brought them outside exploring.

Aisling was growing every day and she loved when the little girl carefully watered her; that was what the cold, sticky thing she felt was. The little girl would use fresh rainwater she had collect from the downpipe outside the pretty bungalow. Every day she would gently sweetly talk and sing to Aisling and her pals.

Aisling's adventures continued for years and the little girl grew alongside her beloved friends. She never missed a single day with them, she brought them everywhere with her on her journeys.

Every so often it was time for a new bigger pot. The little girl would lovingly pack fresh compost and peat into a new bigger pot and then gently lift Aisling from her old pot into the new. She would carefully pack fresh soil around her and water her lovingly.

As the years passed by, Aisling noticed her little girl struggling to carry her and her friends as she was getting so big and heavy.

One day, the little girl carried them outside to the garden and explained to them sadly that she could no longer bring them around with her. She was going to plant them in her garden beside each other.

Aisling felt sad knowing her adventures were coming to an end; but she knew her little girl was struggling to move them, and she did not want to hurt her.

Plus, she still had her friends beside her and Red Squirrel, who was now quite old, was right across from her in his drey.

One bright sunny day, the little girl dug a deep hole with a shovel. She sprinkled some of the chicken pellets into the bottom of the hole and some fresh compost and peat. She lovingly removed Aisling from her pot for the last time and pulled her close to her chest for one final hug and whispered, "I love you".

She then carefully placed Aisling into the hole and packed fresh compost around her. She planted her 3 friends a few meters away around her and they all formed a circle in the corner of the garden.

Chapter 7.

Always Remember
You can be, do & have
anything you want.

Being a tree is an extremely important thing to be. Without trees, there would be no clean oxygen and no clean oxygen means no life on Earth.

Every day, hail, rain, snow or shine, Aisling got to work cleaning carbon monoxide from the air and replacing it with clean oxygen.

She thought of her little girl while she did it. She did it for her.

Her little girl was not so little anymore but had rather turned into beautiful young lady.

She still came outside to Aisling and her friends every day.
Sometimes for just a few seconds, more time for a few hours. She would either climb up their now strong branches and write in her journals, or else gently exercise or relax underneath them.

Aisling especially loved the warm sunny days when their girl and her human friends would spend hours on the purple and navy woven picnic blanket beneath their branches. They would have some beautiful food and drinks and spend hours talking and laughing.

Aisling adored listening to their stories, they fulfilled her sense of adventure.

As time went on, Red Squirrel's children and grandchildren began to use her branches for their own dreys. The warm, fuzzy feeling of new life on her branches was one of her favourite feelings.

She was big and strong and protected her tiny friends from the harsh winter winds and rain.

Years passed. Their girl's parents moved away to a new house and she found a new friend who then moved into the beautiful bungalow with her.

He loved the trees almost as much as the girl and would spend hours sitting and talking, daydreaming, and reading with their girl.

As Aisling grew bigger and stronger, she began to have conkers of her own. She loved every single one of them and would gently hum and sing to them every day.

One autumn, their girl had a daughter.

She was the most beautiful little thing and Aisling and the other trees loved her with all their being.

As she got older, she began exploring in the garden on her own.

One autumn, Aisling's conker babies were talking amongst themselves when Aisling noticed some commotion on one of her great branches.

A quarrel had started amongst the conkers and as Aisling tuned her attention to them and listened in, her heart sank.

"You're just a conker, there's no adventure out there for you" she could hear one of them harshly say to another.

"Now shut up and just accept you're going nowhere" it finished.

At that point, she could hear one of her little babies begin to sob.

Aisling then realised she had never told her little ones of her extraordinary life and all her adventures. She felt saddened by this.

She sent all the love in her down her branch to the little conker.

"My beautiful child, you can do, achieve and have anything you desire.

It does not matter what others think you are or are not or where you started off.

Your dreams are there to be followed.

Life is meant to be fun".

From that day on, Aisling and her pals; acorn, pine tree and hawthorn all spoke to their babies about their amazing adventures, where they had been and what they had done. They never ran out of stories and relished in the joy and love of them.

So, when the day came for the little conker to leave and fall from the branch, can you imagine Aisling's delight when their girl's little girl picked her up in her tiny hand?

The little girl held the conker up high in her outstretched hand towards the sun and declared she had found the most precious of them all.

The mighty protecting conker...

Emma-Jane Leeson is a children's book author from County Kildare, Ireland.

She has penned the popular "The Adventures of Johnny Magory" children's book series.

Emma-Jane is passionate about educating children on Irish heritage and wildlife, in a fun way.

She wrote this story in 2020 to celebrate her daughters sixteenth birthday.

Visit www.JohnnyMagory.com for more information.

Lightning Source UK Ltd.
Milton Keynes UK
UKHW020804051120
372843UK00009B/287